THE HOCKEY SWEATER

30TH ANNIVERSARY EDITION

Story by
Roch Carrier
Illustrations by
Sheldon Cohen
Translated from the original French by Sheila Fischman

TUNDRA BOOKS

I wish to dedicate this story to all girls and boys because all of them are champions. — **R.C.**

To my father, Kelly,
my brother, David,
and my son, Matt, who turns 30 with *The Hockey Sweater*!
I share this book with you. — **S.C.**

Published in Canada by Tundra Books, a division of Random House of Canada Limited,
One Toronto Street, Suite 300, Toronto, Ontario M5C 2V6

Published in the United States by Tundra Books of Northern New York,
P.O. Box 1030, Plattsburgh, New York 12901

Library of Congress Control Number: 2014941832

Library and Archives Canada Cataloguing in Publication information available upon request.

This edition edited by Samantha Swenson
This edition designed by Andrew Roberts
The text was set in Bookman Old Style
www.tundrabooks.com

Printed and bound in China

1 2 3 4 5 6   19 18 17 16 15 14

CREDITS

Page 30, photograph of radio: Courtesy of ECW Press **Page 30**, quote: From interview with Tamara Tarasoff, *"Roch Carrier and the Hockey Sweater,"* Canadian Museum of Civilization **Page 30**, photograph of Roch: Library and Archives Canada, courtesy of Roch Carrier's family (public domain) **Page 32**, book cover: Courtesy of House of Anansi Press **Page 34**, photographs: Courtesy of ECW Press **Page 36**, stills: Reprinted with the permission of National Film Board of Canada. From *The Sweater* © 1980 **Page 38**, photograph: © Martin Girard, Shoot Studio **Page 39**, photograph: by Pierre Beauchemin, courtesy Tundra Archives **Page 40**, photograph: © Jeff Whyte | Dreamstime.com **Page 42**, Eaton's catalogue cover: Used with permission of Sears Canada Inc. **Page 44**, 5 dollar bill: Bank note image used with the permission of the Bank of Canada **Page 45**, photograph: © John Loper, 2012 **Page 46**, photograph: Courtesy of Robert Thirsk and NASA **Page 48**, photograph: © David Barlow-Krelina

BIENVENUE
à
STE. JUSTINE, QUÉ.

pop. 1200

THE
HOCKEY
SWEATER

THANK YOU! These are the first words that come from my heart to my lips at this moment when the anniversary of *The Hockey Sweater* is celebrated.

Thanks to the CBC, which let me write "whatever you want to write."

Thanks to Sheila Fischman, my translator, who made my story accessible to the English-speaking world.

Thanks to my brave French and English publishers.

Thanks to the National Film Board (NFB), which put its support behind making a film out of my story.

Thanks to humble but monumental Sheldon Cohen, the artist who created the film, frame by frame.

Thanks to May Cutler, founder of Tundra Books, who welcomed the idea to put that film into a book for children and did so in a way that only May Cutler could have done.

Thanks, again, to Sheldon Cohen; by the magic of his pencils and brushes, this book, intended for kids, has also been read and is being read by adults who never forget they were kids.

Thanks to composer Abigail Richardson-Schulte who is offering *The Hockey Sweater* story enriched by beautiful symphonic music to thousands and thousands of kids of all ages.

Thanks to teachers and librarians who use the story to attract kids to books, to motivate them into writing, to teach them French or English.

Thanks to the people who bought this book; they were supporting the other books I was working on.

Thanks to the readers who took the time to share with me their personal experiences connected with this little book.

Finally, thanks to all of you who will keep this story alive in the future: reading the book, reading it to children and grandchildren, watching the NFB film, listening to the symphonic adaptation. You are giving me much more than I gave you. Thank you.

ROCH CARRIER

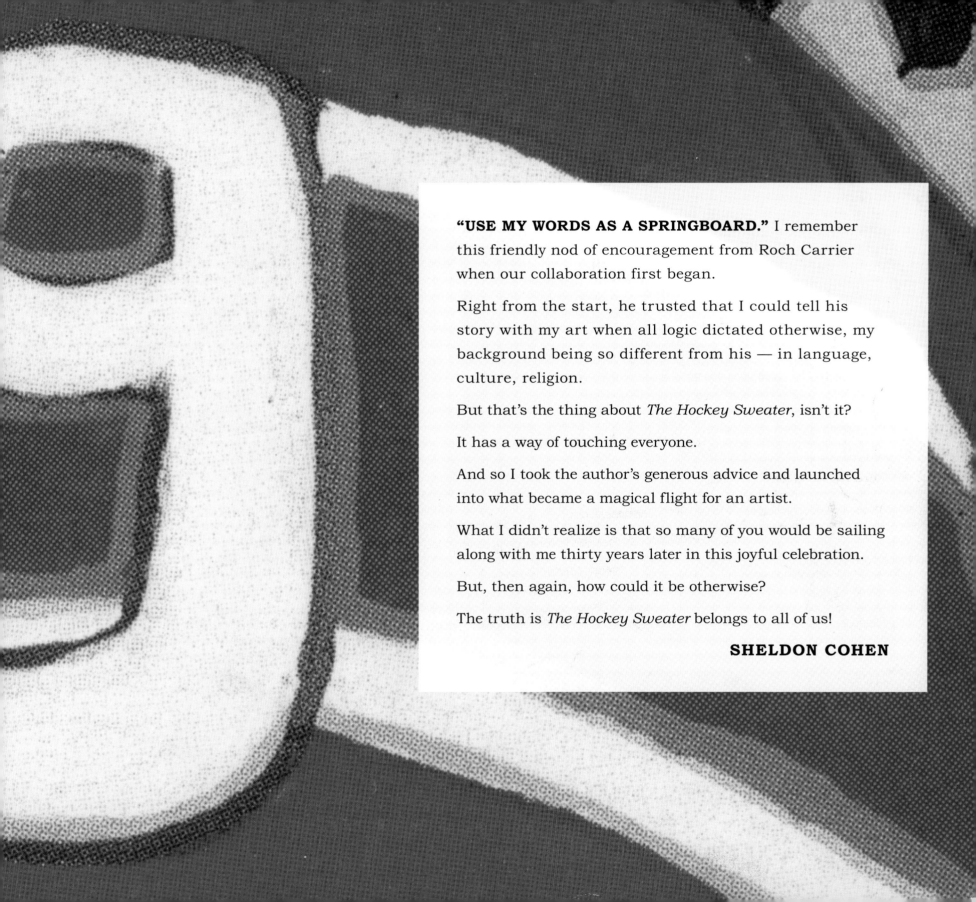

"USE MY WORDS AS A SPRINGBOARD." I remember this friendly nod of encouragement from Roch Carrier when our collaboration first began.

Right from the start, he trusted that I could tell his story with my art when all logic dictated otherwise, my background being so different from his — in language, culture, religion.

But that's the thing about *The Hockey Sweater*, isn't it?

It has a way of touching everyone.

And so I took the author's generous advice and launched into what became a magical flight for an artist.

What I didn't realize is that so many of you would be sailing along with me thirty years later in this joyful celebration.

But, then again, how could it be otherwise?

The truth is *The Hockey Sweater* belongs to all of us!

SHELDON COHEN

The winters of my childhood were long, long seasons. We lived in three places — the school, the church and the skating-rink — but our real life was on the skating-rink. Real battles were won on the skating-rink. Real strength appeared on the skating-rink. The real leaders showed themselves on the skating-rink.

School was a sort of punishment. Parents always want to punish their children and school is their most natural way of punishing us. However, school was also a quiet place where we could prepare for the next hockey game, lay out our next strategies.

As for church, we found there the tranquility of God: there we forgot school and dreamed about the next hockey game. Through our daydreams it might happen that we would recite a prayer: we would ask God to help us play as well as Maurice Richard.

I remember very well the winter of 1946.
We all wore the same uniform as Maurice
Richard, the red, white and blue uniform of
the Montreal Canadiens, the best hockey
team in the world. We all combed our hair
like Maurice Richard, and to keep it in
place we used a kind of glue — a great deal
of glue. We laced our skates like Maurice
Richard, we taped our sticks like Maurice
Richard. We cut his pictures out of all the
newspapers. Truly, we knew everything
there was to know about him.

On the ice, when the referee blew his
whistle the two teams would rush at
the puck; we were five Maurice Richards
against five other Maurice Richards,
throwing themselves on the puck. We were
ten players all wearing the uniform of the
Montreal Canadiens, all with the same
burning enthusiasm. We all wore the
famous number 9 on our backs.

How could we forget that!

One day, my Montreal Canadiens sweater was too small for me; and it was ripped in several places. My mother said: "If you wear that old sweater, people are going to think we are poor!"

Then she did what she did whenever we needed new clothes. She started to look through the catalogue that the Eaton company in Montreal sent us in the mail every year. My mother was proud. She never wanted to buy our clothes at the general store. The only clothes that were good enough for us were the latest styles from the Eaton's catalogue. My mother did not like the order forms included in the catalogue. They were written in English and she did not understand a single word of it. To order my hockey sweater, she did what she always did. She took out her writing pad and wrote in her fine schoolteacher's hand: "Dear Monsieur Eaton, Would you be so kind as to send me a Canadiens' hockey sweater for my son, Roch, who is ten years old and a little bit tall for his age? Docteur Robitaille thinks he is a little too thin. I am sending you three dollars. Please send me the change if there is any. I hope your packing will be better than it was last time."

Monsieur Eaton answered my mother's letter promptly. Two weeks later we received the sweater.

That day I had one of the greatest
disappointments of my life! Instead of the
red, white and blue Montreal Canadiens
sweater, Monsieur Eaton had sent the blue
and white sweater of the Toronto Maple
Leafs. I had always worn the red, white and
blue sweater of the Montreal Canadiens.
All my friends wore the red, white and blue
sweater. Never had anyone in my village
worn the Toronto sweater. Besides, the
Toronto team was always being beaten by
the Canadiens.

With tears in my eyes, I found the strength
to say: "I'll never wear that uniform."

"My boy," said my mother, "first you're going
to try it on! If you make up your mind about
something before you try it, you won't go
very far in this life."

My mother had pulled the blue and white
Toronto Maple Leafs sweater over my head
and put my arms into the sleeves. She
pulled the sweater down and carefully
smoothed the maple leaf right in the middle
of my chest.

I was crying: "I can't wear that."

"Why not? This sweater is a perfect fit."

"Maurice Richard would never wear it."

"You're not Maurice Richard! Besides, it's not what you put on your back that matters, it's what you put inside your head."

"You'll never make me put in my head to wear a Toronto Maple Leafs sweater."

My mother sighed in despair and explained to me: "If you don't keep this sweater which fits you perfectly I'll have to write to Monsieur Eaton and explain that you don't want to wear the Toronto sweater. Monsieur Eaton understands French perfectly, but he's English and he's going to be insulted because he likes the Maple Leafs. If he's insulted, do you think he'll be in a hurry to answer us? Spring will come before you play a single game, just because you don't want to wear that nice blue sweater."

So, I had to wear the Toronto Maple Leafs sweater.

When I arrived at the skating-rink in my blue sweater, all the Maurice Richards in red, white and blue came, one by one, and looked at me. The referee blew his whistle and I went to take my usual position. The coach came over and told me I would be on the second line. A few minutes later the second line was called; I jumped onto the ice. The Maple Leafs sweater weighed on my shoulders like a mountain. The captain came and told me to wait; he'd need me later, on defence.

By the third period I still had not played.

Then one of the defencemen was hit on
the nose with a stick and it started to bleed.
I jumped onto the ice. My moment had come!

The referee blew his whistle and gave me a
penalty. He said there were already five
players on the ice. That was too much!
It was too unfair! "This is persecution!"
I shouted. "It's just because of my blue
sweater!"

I crashed my stick against the ice so hard
that it broke.

I bent down to pick up the pieces. When I got up, the young curate, on skates, was standing in front of me.

"My child," he said, "just because you're wearing a new Toronto Maple Leafs sweater, it doesn't mean you're going to make the laws around here. A good boy never loses his temper. Take off your skates and go to the church and ask God to forgive you."

Wearing my Maple Leafs sweater I went to
the church, where I prayed to God.

I asked God to send me right away,
a hundred million moths that would eat
up my Toronto Maple Leafs sweater.

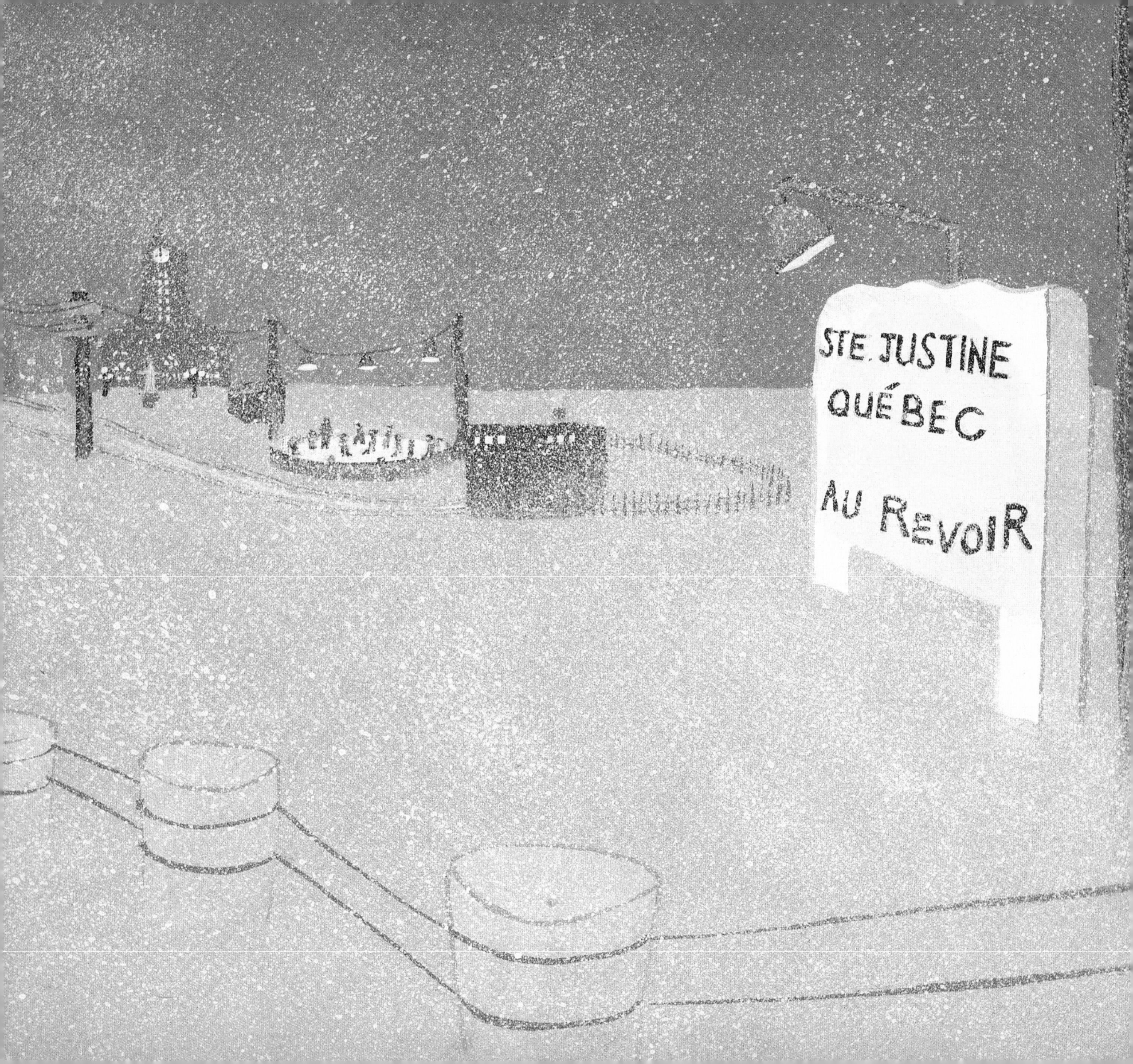
STE. JUSTINE
QUÉBEC
AU REVOIR

THE STORY YOU JUST READ IS TRUE. Roch Carrier, the author of this book, grew up in a very small town in rural Quebec called Sainte-Justine. And just like in the book, hockey was very important in his village. Maybe even more important than school! The hockey rink was where you learned to compete, assert yourself, improve yourself … and show off for girls too. It was where you learned about life. In the 1940s, there weren't three hockey games a night, and there was no television or Internet: just the radio. Every Saturday, families would gather around the radio to hear the game, and at times it felt more important than anything else — even news of the war and of the world outside.

ROCH WAS INSPIRED TO WRITE THIS STORY when he was asked by the CBC to talk about Quebec and the differences at the time between French-speaking and English-speaking Canada. He wrote an essay to read on the air, but he wasn't happy with it (it was pretty boring). Eventually he thought of this particular moment from his childhood and decided to write about it instead.

The family radio

Roch in his dreaded sweater

He once said in an interview that, "I went back to my table and I started to think about when I felt that I was little me, little Roch, not my mother's son, not my father's son, not my brother's brother, not my big brother's brother, all that. When was it that I felt I was really myself? And I remember it was when I put on my skates and my Eaton catalogues on my legs, and I stood up, and I was taller than my mom, and I had a stick in my hands, so I was stronger than my brother, and I felt that I was little me. So I started to write about that and it turned into *The Hockey Sweater* story."

When Roch read it over the air, it received a great response. And that was just the beginning for this little story!

I was once in a public library, talking with the audience after having read *The Hockey Sweater*. A strong man — perhaps a truck driver, a machinery operator — not looking shy at all to be among all the readers — declared: "You know, men are not like women. The women, they talk. They talk to the children. It's easy for them. It's in their blood. Talking to the children, it does not look like it's a man's business. For the men, it's tough ... I have a boy. I don't know what to say to him. So I say to him, 'Let's look at the book.' And the boy brings your book. We look at the pictures, we read some lines, and I tell about when I was playing hockey. He tells me about some games he played, sometimes about school. We talk. Sometimes, it's my boy, now, who asks, 'Pops, can we look at the book?'"

ROCH CARRIER

AFTER BEING READ ON THE CBC,
The Hockey Sweater was published by House of Anansi Press in a short story collection as "Une abominable feuille d'érable sur la glace" or "An abominable maple leaf on the ice." But someone else had heard Roch read it over the air: a producer from the National Film Board of Canada.

The original short story collection

Sheldon's dog K.C. and cat Miriam who appear in the book.

The producer went to an animator named Sheldon Cohen with the idea to make a short film of the story. At first Sheldon wasn't sure — he was English speaking, from a big city and not a great hockey player. Could he really do a good job? He decided he had to try …

After quite a serious business meeting, a gentleman asked me if he could tell me a story that had nothing to do with the meeting. His mother, he said, was suffering with Alzheimer's. The gentleman told me that he had cut out his face and his brothers' faces from the family album and glued them onto the characters in *The Hockey Sweater*. And every day, his mother in her hospital room would ask for the book and turn the pages and perhaps would remember some moments of her life.

ROCH CARRIER

WHEN ROCH SAW SHELDON'S WORK, he knew Sheldon was the perfect person to animate his story. Roch and Sheldon worked together to create *The Sweater*, a ten-minute film based on the original text. They even travelled to Sainte-Justine together so that Sheldon could see the church, the school and, most importantly, the skating-rink. The film was a success, has won many awards and is much loved by fans.

It was after this film was released that Sheldon decided to get in touch with May Cutler, the founder of Tundra Books. He was nervous … what if she wasn't interested in a book version of *The Sweater*? He needn't have worried — she had been wanting to do it since she'd heard it on the radio! So Sheldon and Roch teamed up again to create the book you're holding now.

Sainte-Justine

Many times, I was asked to inscribe a book to a baby who was not born yet. Each time, I had to take a deep breath and think: this is happening to me; I'm being connected to a kid who has not yet arrived on this planet ...

Once, in Stratford, Ontario, a lady came with three copies of *The Hockey Sweater* and asked me to sign a copy for Number 1, a copy for Number 2 and a copy for Number 3.

"Number 1 ... Is he a goalie?" I asked. "And what about number 2? And 3?"

"Oh! They are not born yet. But my daughter is getting married and I expect them to give me three babies!" she replied.

Some months later, I was attending a social event in Ottawa. A lady came to me and asked if I recognized her. "Do you remember? I asked you to sign books for Number 1 ..."

"... Number 2 and Number 3," I continued.

"Well, Number 1 is on his way!" she proclaimed.

ROCH CARRIER

Scenes from *The Sweater*

ALTHOUGH IT WAS THE SAME STORY that was used in the film, it was a different challenge to create the picture book, especially for Sheldon. Animation and illustration work differently, so he had to *think* differently about the art for the book. Creating the illustrations took a whole year, and instead of the 10,000 drawings that made up the animated film, *The Hockey Sweater* has only thirteen. It might seem like doing fewer drawings would be easier, but in fact that's just a different challenge — how do you tell a whole story with only thirteen pictures? It's definitely not easy! But Sheldon found that although he had fewer images to work with, he could fill those images with interesting details and tell more of the story through those details. And each image took many stages before it became the art that you see today.

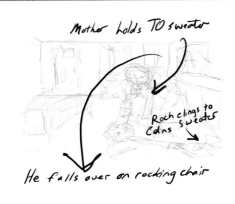

Mother holds TO sweater

Roch clings to Coins

He falls over on rocking chair

Add family watching

Father reading paper - smoking pipe.

Add details:

calendar   clock

kids outside window

cookie jar

Roch's expression not working

Cover face with arm (solves problem)

Clean up light blue lines with dark blue lines.

Create final layout to colour in.

The fun part!!!

Roch Carrier

"I always thought it appropriate that Americans put God on their currency while we Canadians put hockey on ours. And it seems even more appropriate that, for years, the homage to hockey on our five-dollar bill was a quote from Roch Carrier's *The Hockey Sweater*. For many Canadians, our chosen place of worship is the hockey rink, and if the Canadian religion has a Bible, it is this children's tale that is both ageless and for all ages."

ROY MacGREGOR
children's book writer and journalist;
Hockey Hall of Fame print media honoree

"*The Hockey Sweater* will always stand the test of time. It shows the passion that Canadians have for the great sport of hockey and also shows that we can learn valuable life lessons through hockey. It's a book for all ages. One of my favourite hockey books of all time."

CASSIE CAMPBELL-PASCALL
only Canadian athlete to captain
two Olympic gold medal–winning teams

"*The Hockey Sweater* brings back all the memories and nostalgia of why I play this game that I love so much."

HAYLEY WICKENHEISER
four-time Olympic gold medal–winning hockey player

THE ROCKET

If hockey was the most important thing to young Roch and the people in his town, then the most important *person* had to be Maurice Richard: the Rocket. But who was Maurice Richard? Richard played for the Montreal Canadiens for eighteen seasons. His number, 9, was retired in 1960. He was the first NHL player to score 500 goals in a career. He was also the first player to score 50 goals in one season. He and his teammates won five consecutive Stanley Cups — and eight in total over his career. But the Rocket meant more than that. He was tough and talented, but he was also a humble family man from the same background as those who cheered for him. To French Canadians and all Canadians, he was a hero. Roch got to meet his hero, and in 1984, the Rocket presented him with a brand-new Montreal Canadiens sweater — with the number 9 on the back, of course!

Roch and the Rocket

THE TEAMS

The teams in this book, the Montreal Canadiens and the Toronto Maple Leafs, are still two of the best in the National Hockey League. But back then, the NHL looked pretty different. There were only six teams in the league in 1946: Boston Bruins, Chicago Black Hawks, Detroit Red Wings, Montreal Canadiens, New York Rangers and Toronto Maple Leafs. There were sixty games in a season. And the rivalry between the Leafs and the Canadiens was, and still is, fierce. The two teams have played each other close to 800 times. Montreal has won twenty-four Stanley Cups, the most in the league; Toronto has won thirteen, second most in the league. At the time this book was set, the rivalry unfolding on the ice also represented the rivalry between Canada's two biggest cities and the differences between French and English Canada. They were the only two Canadian teams in the NHL, and you only need to read about Roch's reaction to his new sweater to know that this rivalry was taken very, very seriously!

"One of the most beloved of all Canadian stories is *The Hockey Sweater* by Roch Carrier. When Roch and I were little boys, there weren't thirty NHL teams — only six. And there weren't seven Canadian teams — only two, the Toronto Maple Leafs and the Montreal Canadiens. And when Roch was growing up in his tiny village in Quebec, there was no Internet and no TV, only radio. So Roch, like almost every other Canadian of the time, never actually saw the Toronto Maple Leafs or Montreal Canadiens play; he only heard about them. He dreamed them. He fantasized about them. And for the young Roch and his buddies, there was no greater hero than Maurice Richard; Maurice, the Rocket, was the best of them all!

And if you loved the Montreal Canadiens, you — and I know I'm not supposed to say this — *hated* the Toronto Maple Leafs. And if you loved the Leafs, well … you know the rest. And if that Canadian team you loved was out of the playoffs, and that other Canadian team was playing some dreaded American team for the Stanley Cup, you'd cheer for the only Canadian team left — right? Forget it! Not a chance!!

Well, some years after little Roch had become a much bigger Roch, he wrote this perfect little story."

KEN DRYDEN, former Montreal Canadiens goalie, president of the Toronto Maple Leafs,
Member of Parliament and Cabinet Minister

THE EATON'S CATALOGUE

When you need new clothes, you can probably go to a store in the mall or order online. But back in 1946, the Internet wasn't invented yet and clothing stores were rare. Big department stores, such as Eaton's, were only located in cities like Toronto and Winnipeg. For a lot of people, it was a long trip into the city just to go shopping if they didn't want to buy their clothes at the local general store. At that time, almost 50 percent of Canada's population lived in rural areas, so companies like Eaton's sent out catalogues to make sure that anyone in Canada, regardless of where they lived, could buy from them. But it was a long and agonizing wait for those new clothes to come, especially hockey sweaters! Now, only 20 percent of Canada's population lives in rural areas, so catalogues aren't as important. But at the time, they were a staple in every Canadian home. Eaton's catalogues also served another purpose: Roch and his friends used to strap them onto their legs as shin pads when they played hockey!

EATON'S OF CANADA

Fall and Winter 1948-1949

"In 1984, at a children's lit conference in Calgary, I met an American illustrator who was eager to learn about Canadian children's books, so I sent her a box filled with some of my favourites, *The Hockey Sweater* included. Since then, I've sent out numerous parcels, always beginning with what I consider the quintessential Canadian picture book and, whenever possible, I've included the NFB animated version so people can hear the story as it is meant to be heard: in Roch Carrier's inimitable voice. Well, maybe not that inimitable. I once travelled on a train through northern B.C., listening to a VIA Rail conductor and a burly, tattooed CN engineer, in the club car late at night, recite *The Hockey Sweater* text, line by line — in Carrier's distinctive French-Canadian accent. It was a surreal experience — a thoroughly Canadian one! — to watch two trainmen from the West recite, from memory, an iconic Quebec story they had grown to love after hearing it every Christmas on CBC radio, in the author's voice."

BERNIE GOEDHART
Children's book reviewer at *The Gazette* in Montreal

"*The Hockey Sweater* is beloved and passes from one generation to another because, quite simply, it is a perfect picture book. It is the happy marriage of boisterous illustrations that tell their own tale and a poignant, endearing story written by a master. A gem filled with humour and passion."

PAULETTE BOURGEOIS, writer

"If you call yourself Canadian you better have this book in your house! Everything about this Canadian hockey classic, right down to the highly anticipated arrival of the annual Eaton's catalogue, takes me back to my 1950s childhood. Blue or rouge — it was every kid's dilemma. No surprise then that there's blue or red, or both, in all seven Canadian team jerseys today."

PETER MANSBRIDGE
Chief correspondent of *CBC News*

"After 30 years, *The Hockey Sweater* remains an iconic depiction of a truly Canadian experience; it speaks to a passion for hockey and our country shared from coast to coast to coast.

Today, Canadians who were once raised reading and re-reading this brilliant book can share it with their own children, passing on this tale that is so relatable to Canadians across the country.

As a Habs fan, I am proud that Mr. Carrier's story has had such a tremendous impact on Canadians over the past three decades. Many years ago, *The Hockey Sweater* embodied for me the friendly Montréal-Toronto hockey rivalry, and our hometown hero, Maurice "Rocket" Richard.

As a father of future Habs fans, I am delighted that this literary treasure will continue to find its place in the hearts of Canadian children for generations to come."

JUSTIN TRUDEAU
Leader of the Liberal Party of Canada and
Member of Parliament for Papineau

"*The Hockey Sweater*, c'est Canada. No book I've read better captures the feel of winter, the joy of a childhood spent on the ice. Of course, the spectres of family, faith and politics lurk in the background, and that's the genius of this story. It is ageless and timeless."

KEVIN SYLVESTER, author, illustrator, broadcaster

Art by Kevin Sylvester

SINCE ITS PUBLICATION, *The Hockey Sweater* has gathered fans from coast to coast across Canada. It has sold more than 300,000 copies.

The book can be found in some other special places too. *The Hockey Sweater* was given to Prince William, Duke of Cambridge, as an official gift from Canada when he visited as a boy. And in 2013, it was given to his son, Prince George of Cambridge, also as an official gift from Canada. Perhaps the Queen has read it to Prince George before bed!

A small part of the story was also in the pockets of every Canadian from 2001 to 2012: the first lines from the book were featured on the five-dollar bill.

THE STORY MADE IT ONTO THE STAGE, TOO!
There is a symphony based on the book, composed by Abigail Richardson-Schulte. Roch narrates, and the premiere performance was introduced by former Montreal Canadiens goaltender Ken Dryden. The symphony was co-commissioned by the Toronto Symphony Orchestra, the National Arts Centre Orchestra and the Calgary Philharmonic Orchestra.

Roch and the symphony

SO IT'S BEEN IN A PALACE, in pockets and on stage. But it didn't stop there — this book has been to space, too! Astronaut Robert Thirsk brought the English and French versions of the story to the International Space Station.

Where will it go next?

As a child, I was fascinated by heroes from the comic strips in the weekend newspaper. After school, during vacations, I was flying like Superman, I was phoning through my imaginary wristwatch like the detective Dick Tracy and I was exploring unknown worlds like Buck Rogers or Jacques le Matamore (Brick Bradford). Once I undid a little wall my dad had built in his garage to take four planks which became my own rocket. Don't tell me I did not fly with this technology! You might hear more than you wish about my travels into the unknown space.

One day, sixty-four years after those adventures, I got an email from the International Space Station, accompanied by beautiful photographs of the sky and of our little planet. There was also a photograph of the Canadian astronaut Robert Thirsk, busy reading *The Hockey Sweater*.

When he was back on earth, and in Ottawa, astronaut Robert and astronaut Roch read *The Hockey Sweater* together to kids who wanted to know everything about space and about hockey.

ROCH CARRIER

Robert and *The Hockey Sweater* in space

"Astronauts are advocates for literacy. We could not perform our jobs in space if we did not read and write well. For this reason, I was happy to bring copies of *The Hockey Sweater* and *Le Chandail de Hockey* aboard the International Space Station during my six month expedition in 2009. These iconic books exemplify the joy of reading and the regional rivalries that bring our nation together around our winter passion."

ROBERT THIRSK, astronaut

"After 30 years, Roch Carrier's beloved children's book *The Hockey Sweater* still touches the hearts of Canadian hockey fans, young and old.

This short story, born in small-town Quebec, is undeniably a Canadian classic."

THE RIGHT HONOURABLE STEPHEN HARPER,
Prime Minister of Canada

EMBRACING YOUR INNER SCRIBBLE

Are there things that scare you — snakes, spiders, heights?

It may sound strange, but for an artist, one of the most threatening fears can be a blank canvas!

What if I don't know what to paint? What if what I do paint isn't good enough?

These questions filled my mind when I took up the task of illustrating *The Hockey Sweater*.

Luckily, I had a simple solution.

I told myself "Just go for it. Whatever's there, just let it out!"

And that's what I did …

SHELDON COHEN

Sheldon and Roch, 2014

Having had so many privileged moments with readers, I'm not sorry anymore for having been such a bad hockey player. Because of that, I can tell to the kids who, too often, have small dreams about their future:

If you're convinced that you're not good at something, try harder. If you don't get better, think that you are good at something else. Then your job is to find what you're good at. You have to try. Try. Try again. Try hard. Try harder. Good luck kids. Remember: luck comes after work.

ROCH CARRIER